The Song of the Whales

I dedicate this book to those who are not afraid
of slight distortions of reality.

—U.O.

Copyright © 2010 Uri Orlev
First published in Hebrew by Keter Publishing House Ltd., 1997.
Published by arrangement with the Institute for the Translation of Hebrew Literature.
First American edition, 2010.

Houghton Mifflin Books for Children is an imprint of
Houghton Mifflin Harcourt Publishing Company.

www.hmhbooks.com
The text of this book is set in Bembo.

Library of Congress Cataloging-in-Publication Data
Orlev, Uri, 1931–
[Shirat ha-livyatanim. English]
The song of the whales / by Uri Orlev ; translated by Hillel Halkin.
p. cm.
Summary: At age eight, Mikha'el knows he is different from other boys,
but over the course of three years as he helps his parents care for his elderly grandfather
in Jerusalem, Grandpa teaches Mikha'el to use the gift they share of making other
people's dreams sweeter.
ISBN 978-0-547-25752-5
[1. Grandfathers—Fiction. 2. Dreams—Fiction. 3. Old age—Fiction.
4. Family life—Israel—Fiction. 5. Jews—Israel—Fiction. 6. Jerusalem—Fiction.
7. Israel—Fiction.] I. Halkin, Hillel, 1939- II. Title.
PZ7.O633Son 2010
[Fic]—dc22
2009049720

Manufactured in the United States of America
DOC 10 9 8 7 6 5 4 3 2 1
4500217775

The Song of the Whales

by Uri Orlev

translated by Hillel Halkin

Houghton Mifflin Books for Children

Houghton Mifflin Harcourt • Boston • New York • 2010

CHAPTER ONE

Things Have Souls, Too

IN AMERICA HIS NAME WAS MICHAEL. In Israel it was Mikha'el. Though he had studied Hebrew in Sunday school, it took months of living in Jerusalem before he said 'Mee–kha–EL' like an Israeli. Even then, his speech was occasionally laughed at. Sometimes it was because of his American accent and sometimes because of a word he confused, like when he said "French flies" instead of "French fries" or "elbrows" instead of "elbows."

Michael lived in Port Washington, a small town on Long Island Sound, in the state of New York. He was an only child and was born when his parents were no longer young and had given up hope of having children and had stopped all the fertility treatments. When they discovered that they didn't quite know what to do with a little boy, they left him to his nannies, who came and went on a regular basis.

When he was nine, his parents decided to move to Jerusalem. It was because of Grandpa, Michael's father's father. His parents explained that Grandpa was very old and that they wanted to spend his last years with him.

"But why can't he come here?"

"He and your dad already had that argument."

"What argument?"

"Grandpa didn't want Dad to leave Israel and become an American."

"Will we stop being Americans when we move there?"

"No. We'll be Israelis and Americans."

During the months in which they prepared to move, Michael heard other versions of the story, sometimes when his mother was on the telephone with her friends and sometimes when she and his father didn't realize he could hear them. Then there was talk of a house "worth a fortune" and a housekeeper plotting to "steal the inheritance." Although Michael wasn't in the habit of asking about what he wasn't meant to know, all this stuck in his mind. And there were things he did ask, such as:

"Will Dad be at the office all day there, too?"

"Yes. All day."

"And you?"

"I have a job with the Israeli Philharmonic."

Michael realized that nothing would be any different. In Israel, too, his father would be occupied with his meat products business, his mother would practice her cello and tour with the orchestra, and he would have to go to school. Would he make friends in Jerusalem? This worried him, because he didn't make friends easily with boys his age.

"Why not?" his mother had once asked him.

"Because they fight."

"With you?"

"No."

"Then what is it?"

"They shout and run around all the time."

"The girls, too?"

"Come on, Mom. No one plays with girls."

"Not even on school trips? We heard there's going to be one."

"I'm not going on it."

"Why not?"

"Because everyone screams and pushes on the bus. And the teacher gives too many orders."

There were other conversations, too.

"Why don't you ask a friend over, Michael? You'll enjoy it."

"I don't have any friends."

"You should have at least one you can talk to."

"What they talk about doesn't interest me. Can't you understand that?"

Michael didn't care about the things that other boys in Port Washington did. He didn't like sports or computer games. He didn't watch everyone's favorite TV programs. He wasn't into hiking, boating, camping, or nature. What he liked was modeling clay. He preferred Plasticine, because it didn't harden and he could change the figures he had made and pretend they had moved. These were his friends, and he liked to stay in his room and play with them or make more of them. Sometimes they talked to him, and he shaped them to match what they had told him or he had told them. He even made a model of himself, looking bigger and stronger than he was, and since he loved large, powerful machines, he built bulldozers and locomotives and put himself in the driver's seat and rode around the table while everyone watched. Some of his figures came from his imagination and others from books he had read. Michael liked to read, too. But reading got you nowhere in school. Being a good athlete, even if it was just at volleyball, and riding horses and breeding puppies were better ways to be popular.

"Why don't you invite a friend from school and show him your collections?"

"Never!" Michael said angrily.

His mother was thinking of his semiprecious stones, old keys, and model boat collections. He certainly couldn't show the boats to the boys in his class. Many of them belonged to the boating club, sailed, and rowed kayaks and canoes. Michael's boats were made of rough pieces of wood nailed together, to which were glued masts, sails, and stays. He used scraps of lumber or plywood that he cut with a jigsaw.

His boats were less models of boats than ideas of boats. They had more to do with his thoughts and feelings than with anything real.

"How come you're making all those boats?" Michael's father had asked.

"I'm going to be a sea captain when I grow up."

"Sea captains have to know arithmetic."

The same exchange took place when Michael stopped building boats and started building bridges.

"How come you're building all those bridges, Michael?"

"I'll be a bridge designer when I grow up."

"Bridge designers have to know arithmetic."

It wasn't just arithmetic that Michael did badly in. He didn't like school in general. That's probably why he played sick and stayed home so often, which didn't bother his mother one bit. She was busy with her music and let Michael do what he wanted.

"I'll bet your friends would love all your clay figures."

"No, Mom. They'd laugh and say I play with dolls like a girl."

"But you make bulldozers and locomotives, too."

"They don't care about that."

"What do they care about?"

"You know."

"But just look at this wonderful motorcycle you made."

"It's not the kind of motorcycle anyone talks about. It doesn't look real. You don't know anything."

"Why don't you join the boating club? You'd enjoy it more than bothering the neighbors."

"I don't bother them." Michael's feelings were hurt.

None of this had the slightest effect. Michael stayed who he was. He didn't invite other boys to his house or take part in their activities, and when he wasn't busy in his room he went to see what was going on at the neighbors'. If anyone was building, renovating, painting, or gardening, he offered to help. Even as a nine-year-old he had a reputation for being a hard worker. He was always welcome and he was glad to pitch in as long as the work was "real." Real work meant that he could use a hammer, screwdriver, saw, or other tool. He had many grown-up friends. He liked grownups better.

Take Mr. Rapp, who owned a store for rough gems that he supplied to jewelers. He and Michael had become friends when Michael had started a stone collection and had gone to Mr. Rapp's store to buy specimens. He saved up his allowance money and was so proud of it that he felt insulted when Mr. Rapp wanted to give him a gift. From then on, though, he dropped by the store on his way home from school every day. He helped dust the shelves and display cases and fetched gems for Mr. Rapp to show the customers. Best of all, he liked watching Mr. Rapp polish the gems. Sometimes he was allowed to make the first cut himself.

Michael also had a collection of old keys, some given to him by the neighbors and some by Mr. O'Grady, the junk dealer. Mr. O'Grady had a red beard and blue eyes and spoke with an Irish brogue. Michael helped him sort the junk that he bought. Some of it was too old to have any use.

"It's from the days when folks lived by candle-light," Mr. O'Grady liked to say. He knew what everything was for and always explained it to Michael with great patience. All the junk was kept in a big shed behind his store.

Michael's love for books came from another friend, Mr. Albert, the bookbinder. Michael had first visited the bindery with his mother, who had brought Mr. Albert some musical scores. Mr. Albert had said he would bind them as a favor, even though it wasn't his line of work. His specialty was restoring old leather bindings for museums and libraries that brought him their rare books. When the scores were ready, Michael's mother had sent Michael to pick them up.

"Just hold this thread for a second," said Mr. Albert, who was having trouble sewing something.

Michael stayed so long that his worried mother phoned Mr. Albert to ask where he was. After that, he looked in on Mr. Albert often to watch him work and to help with what he could. Mr. Albert not only liked to read books, he liked to touch them, smell them, and turn their pages. If Michael was in the bindery when an especially handsome old volume arrived, Mr. Albert let him hold it and always said:

"Let your hands feel it, Michael. It's not just some old thing. It has a soul."

At first, Michael didn't know what Mr. Albert was talking about.

"A book that has been handed down from generation to generation," Mr. Albert explained, "has had its pages touched by so many fingers and has been loved and cried over by so many people that it has a life of its own."

When he lay in bed before falling asleep that night, Michael still felt moved by those words.

"I'm going to be like Mr. Albert and never get married," he later told his mother.

"Don't you want children?"

"No."

"Why not?"

"Because they'll poke around in my things," Michael had said, making his mother laugh.

Whenever Mr. Albert made himself coffee, he made some for Michael, too. He drank his coffee black and unsweetened but put three cubes of sugar into Michael's.

Michael would have been glad to have made friends with yet another person he had met when he and his mother had brought her cello to be fixed. His eyes had opened wide when they had entered the man's workshop. Before Michael could return there, however, he was informed that he was going to Israel. That same day, he told Mr. Albert about his grandfather and the house in Jerusalem that they were moving to from Port Washington.

"I'll be back, though," he promised. "I'll come to visit my friends."

"What does your grandfather do?"

"He's very old," Michael said.

"And before that?"

"He was an antique dealer." This was something Michael remembered hearing.

"Perhaps," Mr. Albert said thoughtfully, "he'll be your friend, too. I'll bet he knows something about the souls of things."

That day Michael went home early and looked at his father's photograph album. He studied each one of the old pictures of his grandfather, who had argued with Michael's father about America.

CHAPTER TWO

Grandpa and the Kept Housekeeper

IT WAS MICHAEL'S GOOD LUCK that his family arrived in Israel two weeks before the summer vacation, so that he didn't have to start school at once. He only had to go with his mother to register for fourth grade and meet his teacher. When she invited him to meet his future classmates, he declined.

"After the vacation," he said.

Michael liked his grandfather from the minute he set eyes on him. Grandpa was taller than he looked in the photographs and not so old as Michael had imagined. Though he rose from his chair with difficulty, he walked and spoke briskly. He didn't ask Michael about his school in Port Washington or his favorite subjects. He just looked at him as if trying to guess something and smiled. Michael smiled back.

Raphael Hammerman lived in a large, stately house facing Jerusalem's old walled city. Grandma Dora was no longer alive and Grandpa lived with a housekeeper named Madame Saupier who came from France. Madame Saupier served tea and cookies with a sour face. Michael looked at her curiously. Although she was a big, hefty woman, she didn't look like a thief to him. But perhaps there was more than one way to steal an inheritance.

That first Friday evening, Grandpa was their guest for their Sabbath dinner. He came by himself. They hugged and kissed. Only when they sat down to eat did Michael's father remember that Grandpa was a vegetarian. Michael's mother apologized. Grandpa ate some salad and the vegetables that went with the meat, and Michael's mother made him an omelet.

"Grandpa, how come you came by yourself?" Michael asked, to everyone's embarrassment.

There was silence.

"Perhaps Grandpa's housekeeper didn't want to come," Michael's mother said after a while.

"Perhaps she wasn't invited," said his grandfather.

A few weeks went by without seeing Grandpa again. He didn't visit them and they didn't visit him. They might as well have still been in America.

"She's got him under her thumb," Michael's father remarked one evening.

"Shhh," Michael's mother said.

Michael was bored at home. One day he asked his mother if he could visit his grandfather.

"Of course," she said.

It was the first time he rode an Israeli bus by himself.

Michael took an instant dislike to Grandpa's housekeeper. When he rang the front bell, she peeked out a second-floor window without coming to the door, unaware he had seen her. He waited awhile and pressed the bell longer and harder. In the end, she let him in with a frown after looking him over from head to toe—for what, he had no idea.

"Is my grandfather home?" Michael asked.

"Yes, just a minute." She stood blocking his way. "Leave your shoes by the door."

She handed him an old pair of Grandpa's slippers, led him to the kitchen balcony, and carefully brushed off his clothes. Then she made him wash his hands in the bathroom. Only then did she tell Mr. Hammerman he had a visitor.

Michael would have left on the spot had his grandfather not seemed glad to see him and offered to take him on a tour of the house. It had three floors, each with several wings. Some were locked and sealed off. Still, there was enough to see in the others for a whole slew of visits. Michael couldn't get over all the collections and objects that were everywhere, each with a story of its own.

Best of all was Grandpa himself. He reminded Michael of his friends from Port Washington. In a glass cabinet he kept some battered old toys and games that couldn't be touched or played with because they were all that was left of his childhood. Grandpa's childhood seemed to Michael to have been at least a thousand years ago. In another cabinet were a uniform and some medals from the time Grandpa had been a soldier in the Jewish Brigade.

"When was that?"

"In World War Two." Grandpa chuckled to himself.

"What's so funny?"

"The speed with which life turns into ancient history."

From then on, Michael came to see his grandfather frequently and explored the house with him. At first, Madame Saupier went on looking sour. Several times she tried to trick Michael by pretending no one was home. Only when Mr. Hammerman noticed the doorbell ringing was Michael let into the house. One day he caught Madame Saupier in the act and rebuked her sharply.

"I didn't hear any bell," she said, the picture of innocence.

Another time, Madame Saupier left Michael sitting in the living room without telling Mr. Hammerman he was there. Michael had to shout, "Grandpa! Grandpa!" until his grandfather heard him and gave the housekeeper another scolding.

"I'm sorry, Raphael," she said in a sugary voice. "He slipped my mind."

Michael had never heard his grandfather called

by his first name. "I didn't know you were Raphael," he said.

"There are only two people who still call me that," his grandfather said. "Jeanette and sometimes your mother."

"Grandpa, why don't you fire her?" Michael asked.

"I have my reasons." His grandfather gave him a mysterious wink.

Although Michael had no idea what the wink meant, he left it at that.

Once he heard his grandfather grumble:

"Jeanette wants me all to herself."

Michael called Madame Saupier "Soapy." This made his grandfather laugh.

The summer passed and the school year began. Gradually, Madame Saupier grew used to Michael's visits and was nicer to him. One day, when a first autumn rain was falling, he rang his grandfather's bell more hesitantly than usual. He was soaking wet and his shoes were caked with mud. Madame Saupier opened the door, took one look at him, and grinned. He had never seen her do that before and was prepared for the worst, but relaxed when he saw that she meant only to clean him. She pulled off his shoes, set them aside to be polished, and hung up his jacket to dry. Then she rubbed him dry with a towel. He balked only when she tried cleaning his ears and nose with a Q-tip. One ear was as far as she got.

"Let's face it. She's his kept woman," he heard his father say one evening.

Although he didn't know the difference between a housekeeper and a kept woman, Michael imagined it had to do with his grandfather's sometimes taking Soapy to the movies or to a concert or play. He asked his father about it.

"Dad, do people go to the movies with their housekeepers?"

"No, Michael. What makes you ask?"

"Grandpa goes with Madame Saupier," Michael said.

"Maybe that's because she's more kept than a keeper," his mother said with a smile.

Michael made do with her answer. That evening, his parents shut themselves up in their room and talked for a long while. What Michael didn't know was that the more time his grandfather spent with him, the less time Mr. Hammerman had for Soapy. Once, she said in Michael's presence:

"Raphael, are you reading to that boy again? He's become a fixture around here."

"And a very useful one, too," joked Mr. Hammerman, who proceeded to invite Madame Saupier to dinner. "We'll take Mikha'el with us," he said.

"We can take him next week," she said sourly. "This time let's make it just the two of us."

From then on, Mr. Hammerman, his housekeeper, and Michael ate every Tuesday evening at the vegetarian restaurant of his friend Mr. Yerek. Michael, who liked meat, especially chicken breasts fried in bread crumbs, asked why his grandfather didn't eat it.

"Don't you like meat, Grandpa?"

"It isn't moral to kill animals for food" was the answer. "Think what it's like for a cow when you eat her calf."

"She doesn't feel or know anything," Madame Saupier declared.

"No, she doesn't. But we do. That's the difference. And don't think I'm not on to all the steaks you cook behind my back," said Mr. Hammerman.

"I don't deny it," Madame Saupier retorted.

"My mom and dad like meat, too," Michael said.

"That's because I failed to educate your father properly," Mr. Hammerman said.

"But Grandpa, lots of animals are carnivores. That's a word I learned in school."

"The difference between us and the animals, Mikha'el, is that we have minds and can think. There are plenty of things to eat in place of meat."

Michael and his grandfather liked to roam about the house. Sometimes Grandpa took him to one of the locked rooms, where they enjoyed burrowing through forgotten drawers and long-unopened closets. Michael had lots of curiosity and his grandfather answered all his questions with great patience. Sometimes they were surprised to discover a room that no one even remembered was there. The dust and cobwebs didn't faze them and Madame Saupier was delighted to have something new to clean. She scrubbed whatever she could get her hands on—Grandpa, too. That was why, Michael realized, she had been so pleased the day he had walked in from the rain.

Some of the rooms had been display rooms in the days when Grandpa had had his antique business.

Large gold-framed paintings hung on the walls, landscapes and portraits of rich gentlemen and ladies with wide-brimmed hats and strange hairdos, who stared at Michael even when he tried to evade their gaze. Madame Saupier cleaned them with a feather duster. There was also a room of old musical instruments that Michael was not allowed to touch except for an ancient gramophone like one he had seen at Mr. O'Grady's. It had a handle that could be cranked, a stylus that resembled a needle, and a large brass trumpet that Madame Saupier made gleam like gold. When Michael learned to fit the stylus into its cartridge and lower the arm onto an old record, it made squeaky music. The records had a worn, hollow sound. They made Grandpa grab hold of Madame Saupier, even if she was holding a broom or a rag, and dance what he called "the squeaky waltz" with her.

Another room was full of machines. Michael liked two of them especially, an old Singer sewing machine and an ancient knife grinder that stood on four wheels. Their metal parts were set in carved wood frames. Mr. O'Grady, Michael thought, would have loved them. Each had a foot pedal that Michael was permitted to work up and down.

"Grandpa," he asked, "could you photograph the sewing machine and knife grinder for Mr. O'Grady?"

"Who's that?"

"A friend of mine."

Michael told his grandfather about his friend's junkyard and said:

"I'll bet he never saw anything like these."

Grandpa agreed. Michael wrote a letter that said:

Dear Mr. O'Grady,

I'm sending you photographs of two very old machines. You may never have seen anything like them. My grandpa also has an old gramophone like yours and all kinds of other things from the days when folks lived by candlelight. I'm fine and spending a lot of time with my grandpa.

Yours truly,
Michael Hammerman

An answer soon arrived.

Dear Michael,

Thank you very much for your letter and for the lovely photographs that your grandfather took for me. I haven't seen a knife grinder like that in quite a while.

Yours truly,
Kevin O'Grady

In yet another room with wood-paneled walls stood an old piano, its black lacquer showing a reddish sheen in the sunlight streaming through the window. Michael liked to listen to his grandfather play it. Sometimes Grandpa played happy tunes and sometimes sad ones. He also played children's songs, some of which Michael remembered from nursery school. Others he had never heard before. They came from Grandpa's childhood. Michael liked them best of all, mainly because Grandpa sang when he played them.

The piano room had a large stereo set, too. Its big records looked like dishes, not at all like his parents' compact disks. The player had blinking red and green lights and thin black arrows that squirted back and forth in narrow, brightly lit windows. Near the record player were shelves of records, each in a colorful jacket. Some were so old that the turntable had to revolve at a dizzying speed to play them. Sometimes, when Grandpa put on a record for Michael, Madame Saupier joined them and sat there listening while forgetting her cleaning. From time to time she took the records from their jackets, washed them, and carefully dried them with paper towels.

There was also a room called the library. Michael and his grandfather were very fond of it. It had a soft easy chair so large that Michael practically disappeared in it. His grandfather would sit facing him in another chair and read Hebrew stories to him. If there was a word that Michael didn't understand, his grandfather explained it. Madame Saupier liked the library, too, since books, as she observed, gathered dust and had to be wiped. The shelves reached from floor to ceiling. Some held large leather-bound volumes with trimming and gold letters.

"These are like the books Mr. Albert gets to repair," Michael told his grandfather.

"I thought it was Mr. O'Grady."

"No, Grandpa. Mr. Albert is a different friend."

"Didn't you have friends your own age?" Grandpa wondered.

"No."

"Then what did you do all day long?"

"Things," Michael answered. He didn't say what things and his grandfather didn't ask.

"When our container comes from America, I'll show you my collections," he promised. Then he sat down to write another letter to a friend.

Dear Mr. Albert,

You were right. My grandpa knows all about the souls of things.

Yours truly,
Michael Hammerman

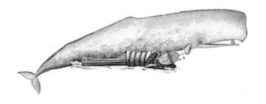

Chapter Three

Wednesday's Secret

ONE OF MICHAEL AND HIS grandfather's favorite activities was walking in the city. Mr. Hammerman loved Jerusalem's old streets and neighborhoods as much as he loved all the old objects and furniture in his big home. He knew the city like the back of his hand. Often he took Michael to some new spot and told him an interesting story about it. On the way, Michael would stop to look at every construction site that they passed. He was fascinated by the cranes that stood on one leg, lifting huge weights with their muscular arms. Although he would never have hurt his grandfather by admitting it, he liked construction sites better than history.

One day, as they stood looking through a gap in a fence surrounding a new hotel that was going up, Michael said:

"Grandpa, I love cranes so much that I could marry one."

His grandfather burst into laughter and said:

"You might not be able to marry a crane, but you could operate one."

"Do you really think so?"

"Of course. Any grownup can learn to be a crane operator."

"Grownups . . ." Michael sighed. "But I'm still a child."

"Let me think about it," said his grandfather.

That winter, Soapy let Michael light the fireplace in the living room. Each time he came to visit, he brought wood from the storeroom, carrying it on his shoulder like a construction worker. He built a base of crumpled newspapers and dry twigs and laid on it the pine and olive branches whose smell his grandfather loved, exactly as Grandpa had taught him. He was very proud of his new duty and wished his parents had a fireplace, too. He would have visited his grandfather in the stormiest weather just to make a fire.

One day, he was sitting on the couch facing the fireplace with Grandpa's arm around him. Suddenly, he rose high in a metal cage to the cabin of a crane at a construction site. Settling into the operator's seat, he engaged the levers, swung out the crane's arm, and dropped the lifting cable. The crane towered above the city and he handled it expertly even though he was just a boy. Far below he saw his grandfather, a tiny figure waving to him.

"Grandpa!" he cried, and woke up.

"What happened, Mikha'el?" Grandpa asked with a sly smile, his arm still around him.

He was getting used to his name being said that way. "I had a wonderful dream," he said thoughtfully. There was something suspicious about his grandfather's smile. Did Grandpa know what he had dreamed?

The first time Grandpa took Mikha'el down to the workroom in the basement, he could see that his grandson was good with his hands. Grandpa repaired his antique furniture himself. Sometimes he had to rebuild it from scratch. The workroom had power saws, drills, chisels, hammers, mechanical planes, and fret saws, plus drawers full of nails and screws arranged by types and sizes. There was an assortment of lumber, boards, beams, and logs, each with a label. Many of the names were new to Mikha'el.

"When you repair antique furniture," his grandfather explained, "you have to use the same wood it was made from."

One day a week was set aside for repairing furniture. Every Monday they went down to the workroom. If Grandpa was stripping down two old closets to make one, Mikha'el would pull out the nails from the leftover wood for him to use somewhere else. Grandpa had an almost religious awe of these nails, which a smith had forged hundreds of years ago from red-hot iron. Mikha'el felt proud of his grandfather when rich customers or tourists still occasionally came to make a purchase and he lectured them about its origins.

"Your grandpa has hands of gold," his mother once said to him, glancing with a sigh at an electric socket that had come loose from the wall. "It's a shame he didn't pass them on to your father."

Once, too, Mikha'el told his father, who was trying to fix a picture frame, "Dad, if you flatten that nail with the hammer, it won't split the wood." His father looked up in surprise and asked:

"How do you know?"

"I learned it from Grandpa."

"I sometimes think you live more with Grandpa than with us," said his father. "Ouch!" he groaned as he hit his finger with the hammer.

Grandpa didn't repair just furniture. If anything broke in the house or the garden, he and Mikha'el brought the tool chest and he fixed it himself. Whenever he grunted or breathed heavily and had to stop to rest, Mikha'el would say worriedly:

"Grandpa, maybe you should get an electrician."

"One of these days I'll have to, but I'll do it myself while I can." His grandfather lapsed into thought. "Maybe I like fixing things so much because I'd really like to fix the world. And for that, it's too late."

The winter passed. It was already spring when Grandpa revealed his secret.

"Come tomorrow, Mikha'el," he said one Tuesday afternoon after walking his grandson home from the restaurant.

"But tomorrow is Wednesday, Grandpa."

"So it is. But come anyway. It's a surprise."

Wednesday afternoons had always been his grand-father's private time during which Mikha'el was not allowed to visit. Although he had asked several times, he had never found out what was so private about it.

Arriving the next day, Mikha'el waited impatiently for Soapy to let him in. To his astonishment, he found his grandfather in front of the bathroom mirror, dressed in dirty old clothes and beat-up shoes and gluing a fake beard to his chin. Soapy handed Mikha'el another pair of old shoes and his grandfather told him to put them on.

"Grandpa, this isn't Purim," Mikha'el said. That was a holiday on which people in Israel dressed up in funny costumes.

"I know," replied his grandfather, clapping an old cap on his head.

Soapy wore her usual clothes. Whatever Grandpa's surprise was, Mikha'el guessed it was just for the two of them. He put on the old shoes and Grandpa went to get the knife grinder from its display room and wheeled it out the front gate while Soapy looked on resignedly with a disapproving, even disgusted expression. Then Grandpa wheeled the knife grinder through the streets of Jerusalem, heading for Me'ah She'arim, a poor and very religious neighborhood not far from where he lived.

"Grandpa, what are you up to?"

"Just be patient, Mikha'el," Grandpa said.

When they reached the narrow streets of Me'ah She'arim, Grandpa slowed down and began to shout:

"Sharpen your knives and scissors! Knives and scissors sharpened here!"

Mikha'el was flabbergasted. Although he had felt that something strange was about to happen, he had never imagined anything like this. But soon his grandfather rose even higher in Mikha'el's esteem as he saw the women of the neighborhood, their heads covered with kerchiefs, flocking from their homes with their utensils. They obviously knew the knife grinder and expected his Wednesday visits. Some came with kitchen knives, others with old shears that had grown dull. Everything had its set price. Although there were customers who tried to bargain, Grandpa wouldn't stoop to it.

"You get the value you pay for," he told whoever argued.

Some of the customers were children whose mothers had sent them with coins tied in a piece of old newspaper. Others were older sisters carrying a baby in their arms while a second child tugged at their skirts. All thronged around, admiring the knife grinder.

From then on, Mikha'el no longer went home from school on Wednesdays. He ran straight to his grandfather's, ate Soapy's vegetarian lunch, put on his old shoes, and set off with Grandpa for Me'ah She'arim, helping to push the knife grinder when it had to be wheeled uphill. After a while they would stop in some little square crisscrossed by laundry lines and surrounded by decrepit houses that looked about to collapse. A few cries from Grandpa and the kerchiefed women came running, followed by curious boys and girls. Mikha'el felt like a sorcerer's apprentice. "Water!" Grandpa would command from time to time, and Mikha'el would hand him a bowl in which to dip the knife or scissors he was sharpening. It made Mikha'el feel important.

At first, all the women and children frightened him. After a while, though, he realized that the children were no different from the ones at school, even if the boys wore yarmulkes and had locks of hair curled around their ears and the girls dressed in blouses with long sleeves. They treated him respectfully despite his not looking like them, and he could see how they appreciated Grandpa and the real work that he did. Whenever someone thanked Grandpa warmly for being such a good knife grinder, Mikha'el thought:

I guess he's fixed the world a bit after all.

CHAPTER FOUR

Reincarnation

WHEN MIKHA'EL WAS ELEVEN and in fifth grade, Grandpa fell ill and had to be hospitalized for a month. Mikha'el visited him every week with his parents. Madame Saupier stood by Mr. Hammerman's bed, watching over him.

"Now is our chance," Mikha'el's father said to his mother.

Nevertheless they were surprised at how easy it was to convince Grandpa, over Madame Saupier's strenuous objections, to sell his big house and live with them. All the arguments used by his housekeeper to persuade him that he should live out his life with her in his own home got her nowhere.

"You don't have to humiliate me like this, Raphael," she wept. "It's all because of the boy, I know it."

She was right, of course, even if Mr. Hammerman kept his thoughts to himself. It was because of Mikha'el that he had agreed to move in with his son and daughter-in-law. Not only did he love his grandson dearly and want to be near him in the time he had left, there was no other way to test Mikha'el's mettle.

Mikha'el grieved for the old house.

"What will happen to the workroom? And what about the knife grinder and all the tools? And the piano and gramophone?"

"Mikha'el," his grandfather said, "I want to be near you. You know I'm a man of eighty-one."

Yes, Mikha'el thought, *Grandpa is getting old.*

"I'll bring some things with me," his grandfather promised him. "One day they'll be yours."

"The knife grinder, too, Grandpa?"

"Of course. The knife grinder, too."

One day? The thought worried Mikha'el.

Grandpa's lawyers sold the house and most of its

contents in a big public auction that was advertised in the newspapers and even made the end of the TV news. The wealthy Mr. Raphael Hammerman, it was reported, had decided to divide his estate between his family and the woman he had been living with for years. The family's share was bequeathed to them on the condition that Mr. Hammerman's son leave his meat business and engage in something more to his father's liking.

And so Grandpa came to live with them, bringing along some of the gold-framed paintings and a few other items that didn't interest Mikha'el in the least. Even with his grandfather's backing, it wasn't easy to get his mother to agree to store the knife grinder and the work tools in the basement. The big power saws and drills were left behind. The piano, on the other hand, which Mikha'el's mother, according to Grandpa, had "had her eye on for a long time," was welcomed along with the gramophone, now a centerpiece in their living room.

Soapy moved in with them, too.

"She's afraid he'll disinherit her if she leaves him," said Mikha'el's father.

"She honestly loves him," his mother said. "And anyway, maybe he'll change his will and give her half to Mikha'el."

"If you ask me, she's still plotting to . . ."

Noticing Mikha'el approaching, they continued their conversation in a whisper.

Another problem was Mr. Hammerman's vegetarianism. The worries about it were soon dispelled, however, when Madame Saupier took over the cooking and their previous housekeeper was let go. The second floor had four bedrooms, two of which had served as Mikha'el's parents' workspaces. Now his mother took to practicing her cello in the living room and his father moved his files to an office in town, making room for Grandpa and Madame Saupier. Mikha'el kept his old room, while Madame Saupier moved in next door to him with Grandpa on her other side.

Since Madame Saupier no longer had as much to clean, she was obliged to attack the same rooms and targets every day. Enemy number one was Mikha'el's family, and especially Mikha'el himself. She hadn't been living with them for a week when she asked Mikha'el's mother for permission to rid him of the germs he brought home from school by means of a daily bath.

Mikha'el was no longer a baby and put his foot down. It was less embarrassing to agree to take his own bath every night. Opening the faucet wide for Soapy to hear the running water, he wet a bar of soap, a towel, and his toothbrush and smeared lather behind his ears and toothpaste over his mouth. Although he hated the taste of the toothpaste, the smell set Soapy's mind to rest. And it was better than taking a bath.

His explorations in his grandfather's old house were a thing of the past.

"Don't worry, Mikha'el," Mr. Hammerman said. "I've got a surprise in store for you."

Not everything changed for the worse. Grandpa still read aloud to Mikha'el and played music for him, sometimes on the CD set in the living room and sometimes in his bedroom on equipment he had bought. One evening, when Mikha'el came to his grandfather's bedroom to say good night, he found him reading in bed by the light of a bedside lamp.

"I bought a new CD today," his grandfather said. "It's on the table. Would you like to hear it? You might find it interesting."

Mikha'el put the disk in the player and sat on the edge of his grandfather's bed.

"What strange music," he marveled.

"It's a recording of a whale song."

"Real whales, Grandpa?"

Suddenly, he no longer felt like himself, though he was not anyone else he knew, either. Yet the green water he was surrounded by, a great expanse of it, seemed perfectly real. Looking around, he saw he was in an ocean. For a few seconds, he was frightened and couldn't breathe. Then, though, he saw his grandfather. How he knew it was Grandpa he didn't know, because Grandpa didn't look like Grandpa. He had long flippers and a huge tail, and he passed in front of Mikha'el like a spaceship in a science-fiction movie crossing the screen so slowly that it takes a while to realize that it is traveling with the speed of light through infinite space. First a head went by with an enormous mouth and a mischievously winking eye, just like Grandpa's when he told a funny joke. Then came the rest of the body, which seemed endless until at last the great tail appeared, thrashing the water. Grandpa was singing. The melody wasn't like the songs from his childhood. It was so slow that each note reached Mikha'el's ears only after a very long time. Other whales were singing, too, their hulking bodies murky in the sea. And there was another voice, too, close and familiar. Mikha'el wondered whose it was and realized it was his own. He awoke in a fright. He wasn't alone. His grandfather lay beside him in the dim glow of the lamp.

"Grandpa?"

"Yes, Mikha'el."

"How did I get here?"

"Don't you remember? You fell asleep next to me."

"No, I don't," Mikha'el said in bewilderment. "Did you cover me with your blanket?"

"It wasn't me," Grandpa said. "It was the whale."

He winked as in the dream.

The room was quiet. The CD had stopped playing long ago.

"Grandpa, we were whales," Mikha'el said excitedly.

"I know," his grandfather said.

"It was the strangest thing, Grandpa," Mikha'el went on dreamily as if he were still asleep. "Everyone was a whale."

"I know," his grandfather repeated. "Maybe we were whales in another incarnation."

"Was it the recording?"

"The recording might have caused us to remember what we once were."

"Who was dreaming, you or me?"

"I was. But I took you into it."

"How?"

"That's something I can do."

"What's an incarnation, Grandpa?"

His grandfather explained the ancient belief in the rebirth of souls.

"Do you think it's true?"

"Everything is possible until proved wrong."

"Grandpa, I loved dreaming with you. Can you take me into more dreams?"

"Yes, if you'll let me."

"Was this your surprise?" Mikha'el asked.

Again the answer was "Yes."

Mikha'el kissed his grandfather good night and went to his room. Before falling asleep, he kept checking to make sure that he was in his own bed, and he felt safe only when he awoke there in the morning. Yet his anxiety passed during the day and soon he could only think of what dream he would be in next. He couldn't wait to find out.

That evening, Mikha'el asked his parents about reincarnation. Both said they didn't believe in it.

Dear Mr. Rapp,

Do you believe in reincarnation?

Yours truly,
Michael Hammerman

An answer soon arrived.

Dear Michael,

Yes, I believe in reincarnation. We all miss you here in Port Washington.

Yours truly,
Christopher Rapp

CHAPTER FIVE

Slight Distortions of Reality

FROM THAT NIGHT ON, Mikha'el often fell asleep with his grandfather. He didn't mind the snores, coughs, smells, and wheezes, or the false teeth gleaming in a glass of water on the night table. All that vanished when his grandfather dreamed. Then he was a healthy man with no signs of the unsteady gait, trembling hands, or heavy breathing that afflicted him when he was awake.

"If you're going to sleep with me, Mikha'el," he said, "watch out for Madame Saupier."

"Why?"

"She won't stand for it. She thinks all children have germs. You have to wait for her to fall asleep first. She sleeps like a log. If you can stay up long enough, she won't hear you passing her room."

"But how will I know she's asleep, Grandpa?"

Mr. Hammerman laughed. "By her snores."

Mikha'el did as he was told. Every night he lay in bed and waited, struggling to keep his eyes open. Although his grandfather had told him to prop his lids up with matchsticks, he knew this was just a joke. Usually he fell asleep, but when he managed to stay awake it was well worth it. First he would hear Madame Saupier leave the bathroom and go to her room. As soon as she would begin to snore, he'd slide out of bed and tiptoe past her open door. True to his word, his grandfather took him into his dreams. Some were short and some long and full of adventures.

One night Madame Saupier discovered Mikha'el half asleep in his grandfather's bed and sent him back to his room.

"You mustn't let him into your bed, Raphael," she warned Mr. Hammerman. "All children carry diseases."

"I can't throw him out when he has a bad dream in the middle of the night."

"He can go to his parents."

"I've already told you they don't permit it. They have funny ideas about raising children. It probably comes from so many years of not having one."

Madame Saupier flushed. Mr. Hammerman had remembered too late that not having children was a sore point with her.

"You'll catch something from him, that's for sure," she said, slamming the door behind her.

If only she could have, Madame Saupier would have lain all night in front of Grandpa's door to protect him, the way slaves lay long ago on the thresholds of their masters. Her old bones, however, weren't made for sleeping on the floor.

"Grandpa, what difference does it make to her?"

"She's jealous."

"Of what?"

"I used to take her into my dreams, too, after Grandma Dora died. Then I stopped."

"Does she know you take me?"

"Goodness gracious, no," his grandfather said. "She doesn't suspect a thing."

"Why 'goodness gracious'?"

"She'd make trouble if she found out."

"What kind of trouble?"

"Who knows? Jealousy is the dark side of love."

Sometimes Grandpa's dreams were more than just dreams. They were, as he told Mikha'el, "slight distortions of reality." Although this was too fancy a phrase for Mikha'el to understand, he grew to like these distortions of reality best of all—better even than his games and collections that had arrived in their container from America.

One dream was especially unforgettable, perhaps because it kept recurring. In it, they were walking toward a house in a woods. His grandfather was holding his hand. It was evening and getting dark, and they were approaching some steps leading to an open, lit doorway. There were people sitting on the steps. More were inside, some in chairs and some sprawled on a couch. A few were gathered by a stove, while others leaned on the windowsills, gazing into the darkness. Mikha'el could remember every one of them, how they all looked, their clothing and hair, and what they did. Each time he dreamed the scene, he was haunted by the same air of mystery, the eerie feeling that he had been there before, even though none of it was familiar. Thinking about it when he was awake, he realized it was part of a longer dream, the rest of which he couldn't remember.

One dream he did remember from beginning to end was of his grandfather's inventing an anti-time machine. The demonstration Grandpa gave was such a success that he was joyously crowned king and emperor. Yet gradually the joy faded, because the years went by and nothing ever changed. The same baby birds went on nesting in the same nests while the same father and mother birds brought them the same worms to eat. The same grandmothers beat the dust from the same rugs in the same windows, and the same children went to the same schools and stayed in the same grades. In the end, everyone grew tired of it. One day Grandpa found Mikha'el in his room, crying bitterly.

"What's the matter, Mikha'el?" he asked. As king and emperor, he could grant his grandson any wish.

"Grandpa," Mikha'el sobbed, "I'll never grow up."

He was still crying when he woke in his grandfather's bed. Grandpa woke, too, and lay there sadly. "At least it wasn't a nightmare," he apologized.

Mikha'el couldn't explain what had made him cry. The problem was that he couldn't make up his mind about which he wanted: to be a big, strong grownup who drove a sports car and wasn't afraid of the monsters in his dreams, or to remain eleven years old forever so that his grandfather wouldn't have to die.

It took a dream about flying to make Mikha'el understand what a "slight distortion of reality" was. He and his grandfather were riding bicycles, pedaling furiously. At first, they rode straight ahead. Suddenly, with a great effort, they took off into the air. This wonder didn't last long. Like baby birds attempting to fly for the first time, they soon fell back to earth. Mikha'el felt a lump of disappointment in his throat. But his grandfather didn't give up. They tried again, and this time their doubts yielded to an invincible feeling of confidence and control. Pedaling easily, they soared high over rooftops and trees. They let go of the handlebars and spread their arms wide over an indescribably beautiful valley beneath them. The pure air and blue skies stretching to the horizon filled Mikha'el's whole being. Yet all at once it struck him that he had never ridden a bicycle before. The next thing he knew, he had fallen out of bed and landed on the floor with a thump. For two weeks he went about with an athletic bandage on his sprained foot.

"Mikha'el, you'll have to learn to ride a bike if you want to dream that dream with me again."

"I will, Grandpa," Mikha'el said.

Despite the protests of Mikha'el's parents, Mr. Hammerman picked up the phone and ordered a bicycle that Mikha'el chose from a catalog. His father and mother were afraid that he was too young and would be run over. Needless to say, neither Mikha'el nor his grandfather breathed a word about why he needed a bike.

It wasn't easy to learn to ride it. The weekend after it arrived, his father ran behind it, holding the seat while Mikha'el pedaled. The second his father let go, though, Mikha'el fell. Then Grandpa suggested a different method. It had stages. The first stage was for Mikha'el to hold the bike with both hands, one on the seat and one on the handlebar, and walk beside it. Mikha'el liked this, because whoever saw him thought he could ride a bike and was just stretching his legs. The second stage was mounting the bike and coasting down a slight grade with his feet scraping the ground, ready to brake with them when he wanted.

It took six weeks of this for Mikha'el to learn. After that, he and his grandfather flew in their dreams with no problem. The bicycles were just a means of getting off the ground and were discarded as soon as Mikha'el and his grandfather were airborne, gliding on the wind with outstretched arms like great birds. When they were ready to land, the bicycles appeared again. By then, though, Mikha'el was usually awake, the joy of flying still on his face. Sometimes they woke together. Grandpa would be smiling, too.

CHAPTER SIX

Maya

ONCE MIKHA'EL COULD RIDE his bike, his grandfather taught him how to take care of it. He showed him how to fix a flat tire and all kinds of other things, such as reengaging a loose chain and adjusting the height of the seat and handlebars.

One day, when his class visited the youth wing of the museum, a classmate named Maya showed them the animals she had made in her sculpture club. Mikha'el loved them. He would have liked to show Maya his own clay figures.

She and another girl shared the desk in front of

him. He couldn't stop staring at her braid. He was familiar with every one of her barrettes, both the old ones she kept using and the new ones that appeared from time to time. One day, though, his heart sank. The braid was gone.

"Maya, how could you have cut your hair?"

The question was out of his mouth before he could stop it. A few children turned around. One smirked. Someone giggled. Mikha'el turned red as a beet.

After this, Mikha'el ignored Maya so completely that the incident was forgotten. Yet once he learned to ride his bike, he often rode it past her house in the hope that she would see him. One day she did.

"Mikha'el, you're just who I'm looking for! Can you fix a flat tire?"

"Yes," he said. "Do you have tools?"

"No, I don't."

"Then come to my house."

"All right," Maya said.

She went off and came back a few minutes later, wheeling her bicycle.

"I have an hour until my lesson," she said.

"What are you studying?"

"Piano. I love it."

"My grandpa plays the piano," Mikha'el said. "He's the one who taught me how to fix bicycles."

They walked their bikes to Mikha'el's house.

"My grandpa moved in with us," Mikha'el said.

"I'd die if mine did," said Maya. "I hate old people. They're so ugly."

Was his grandfather ugly? Mikha'el had never thought about it.

"He came with his housekeeper," he said. "She's our housekeeper now. She cooks for us, too. My dad says she's his kept woman."

"Do you know what that is?"

"I guess it's someone you go to concerts and movies with," Mikha'el said doubtfully. He knew he had said something foolish even before Maya burst out laughing.

"Is that really what you think?"

"No," he said. "I was joking."

"How old is your grandfather?"

"Eighty-one. Maybe more by now."

"Is your housekeeper that old, too?"

"No. She must be about fifty."

"And they actually sleep together?"

"Who?" He didn't follow her.

"Your grandfather and his kept woman."

"Don't be crazy!"

"Then she's not what you think," Maya said knowingly. "That isn't a kept woman."

What would Maya say if she knew that sometimes Mikha'el slept with his grandfather? He didn't think she would believe him. Besides, he could never tell her that his grandfather took him into his dreams or that there were distortions of reality. And yet, if there were one person in the world he could tell, he would want it to be Maya.

He glanced at her. Even the way she wheeled her bike did something to him. It was a good thing, Mikha'el thought, that none of his classmates lived on his street or could see them. He let Maya into their yard and went to get his tools.

"You're a real repairman," Maya complimented him when he had finished pumping up the tire. "Do you know how to raise a seat? This bike is getting too small for me, but my parents won't buy me a new one."

Mikha'el raised the seat and invited Maya into the house.

"I want to show you something," he said. "It's something I made."

He showed her his collection of figures. She was full of admiration.

"They're fabulous, Mikha'el! Why don't you sign up for the sculpture club at the museum?"

"Are there any boys in it?"

"It's mostly girls, but there are some."

"I'll think about it," he said.

As he was walking Maya back to the street, his mother arrived and was surprised to see them.

"Hello," she said. "Are you a friend of Mikha'el's?"

Maya was embarrassed. "We're in the same class."

Mikha'el said goodbye to her and joined his mother.

"Your friend is very nice," she said.

"Cut it out, Mom. She's not my friend. I was just fixing her bicycle."

"Excuse me," said his mother. "I didn't mean anything by it."

That same day Mikha'el told his grandfather how he had fixed a classmate's bicycle. Not just a flat tire. He had also raised the seat and handlebars and straightened some spokes in the wheels.

"Bravo," his grandfather said. "Who's the girl?"

He studied Mikha'el's face.

"Her name is Maya. She makes these great animals from clay. She showed them to our class when we visited the museum."

Mikha'el blushed. Grandpa pretended not to notice.

The next morning Mikha'el told his mother that he wanted to sign up for a sculpture club.

"The boy is growing up," declared his father.

"Maybe he'll be a sculptor," said his mother. "Do you have some particular club in mind?" she asked Mikha'el.

"Yes," he said. "The one in the youth wing of the museum."

"All right," she promised. "I'll register you today."

Grandpa said nothing. He already knew.

Dear Mr. Albert,

I fixed a bike that belongs to a girl in my class. I never thought I'd talk to a girl and now I've fixed her bicycle. Her name is Maya. Mr. Albert, how come you never married?

Yours truly,
Michael Hammerman

CHAPTER SEVEN

The Wolf's False Teeth

A DREAM THAT NEVER FAILED to scare Mikha'el was one in which his grandfather was doubled. Not as in a mirror—there really were two of him. Although it stood to reason that only one of them could be Grandpa, Mikha'el was never able to tell them apart or decide who the impostor was or what he wanted.

Usually, the dream began with all three of them sitting on a park bench. Mikha'el would start a conversation meant to discover who was who, but it never worked. Each grandfather answered just as politely.

No matter how he scrutinized them, they looked exactly the same.

"Are you my real grandpa?" he would ask one man.

"Of course I am, my boy," came the answer.

"Then who are you?" he asked the other.

"I'm your grandpa, my boy. It's really me."

"But who's that sitting next to you?"

"No one."

"You mean you don't see the man next to you?"

The second Mr. Hammerman glanced at the first Mr. Hammerman and said:

"No. No one's there."

"Don't believe him," said the first Mr. Hammerman. "He'll try to convince you, but he's lying. Just listen to that phony oh-so-sweet voice of his. He can't possibly not see me—I'm right here."

Mikha'el could see that for himself. He just didn't know whom to believe.

"Grandpa!" He turned to the second Mr. Hammerman. "How can you not see someone sitting next to you? Stick out your hand."

The second Mr. Hammerman stuck out his hand

so vigorously that it knocked the first Mr. Hammerman off the bench. Mikha'el said angrily:

"You liar! Don't tell me you didn't see him now."

He helped the fallen Mr. Hammerman to his feet. But just when he thought he knew who his real grandfather was, the two men began pulling him in opposite directions. They started to shout and Mikha'el would wake up in a cold sweat. Although only one grandfather was lying beside him in bed, which of the men in the dream was he? Mikha'el would then slip out of his grandfather's bed and run back to his room.

One morning, he looked at his grandfather suspiciously. Was it his real grandpa or the impostor?

"It's really me," Mr. Hammerman said with a mischievous smile. But Mikha'el remembered that the second Mr. Hammerman had smiled the same way in the dream and had said, "It's really me," too.

For four nights in a row he slept in his own room and kept away from his grandfather's bed. On the fifth morning, he plucked up the courage to ask:

"Grandpa, why do you keep having that dream?"

"It beats me," his grandfather answered.

"At least warn me when you're going to dream it."

"I can't," his grandfather said. "It just happens. But there's a way to tell us apart."

"What is it?" Mikha'el asked eagerly.

"My teeth are normal. His are like a wolf's."

"I didn't see any teeth like that."

"That's because they're false teeth. He was hiding them in his pocket."

Mikha'el had to laugh and his grandfather joined him.

"Next time, look for them," Mr. Hammerman said. "And don't worry. I'm looking after you."

Mikha'el nodded worriedly, recalling how the two men had nearly torn him apart.

That night, Madame Saupier went to bed late and Mikha'el fell asleep and didn't wake up until it was time for school in the morning. But the following night found him back on the park bench with the two grandfathers. He decided to give it a try. He got to his feet and told a joke.

"Listen to this. Dan's older brother comes to his mother and says, 'Mom, little Dan just swallowed a cockroach.'

"'Oh, no!' says Dan's mother.

"'Don't worry,' his brother says. 'I made him eat a whole can of cockroach spray.'"

Both grandfathers burst out laughing. Mikha'el tried to look at their teeth. As soon as they saw him, both opened their mouths wide, yanked out their teeth from inside, tossed them high in the air, and caught them before Mikha'el could tell which looked like a wolf's.

"Grandpa, stop it!" Mikha'el shouted.

Neither man stopped. Their gummy mouths roaring with laughter, they kept juggling their false teeth. Mikha'el ran back and forth trying to grab a set of them, or trying at least to get a good look, but the two grandfathers were too tall. The minute he got close to one of them, the man quickly threw his teeth in the air. After a while, they started playing catch on a nearby lawn, tossing the teeth back and forth over Mikha'el's head. It seemed hopeless. Yet suddenly, one of the grandfathers missed and the teeth fell to the ground. The three of them ran to look at them. They looked like wolf's teeth.

"They're his!" shouted the first grandfather.

"No, they're his!" the second shouted.

They grabbed Mikha'el by the arms. He tried to fight free but couldn't and woke up with a scream, biting and kicking.

"Grandpa?"

His grandfather was awake, too.

"I couldn't figure out anything," Mikha'el said crossly.

"You're right," Mr. Hammerman said. "You'll never tell us apart. I know why, too. It's because one of us is the dark side of me."

"You have a dark side?"

"Everyone does."

"Me too?"

"You too."

"I never met my dark side," Mikha'el mused.

"You just never paid it any attention," said his grandfather. "The next time you do something bad, touch your teeth and you'll see they're sharper."

"You're joking, Grandpa," Mikha'el said, touching his teeth. They were the same as always.

CHAPTER EIGHT

Meat Day

As Mikha'el was walking down the street one evening, he spied his parents and his grandfather ahead
of him and ran to catch up. His grandfather looked
surprised to see him.

"What are you doing here, Mikha'el?"

"But Grandpa . . ."

Before he could finish the sentence, his grandfather smiled at him. It wasn't his usual smile. Were
those the teeth of a wolf? They were nearing the
vegetarian restaurant when its owner, Mr. Vitalski,
stepped outside with a sly, sinister look that wasn't at

all like fat, jovial Mr. Yerek's—in fact, even his name had changed. On the door he hung a large sign that said in black letters:

MEAT DAY

"That's very interesting," Mikha'el's mother said.

"Very," said his father. "I'm famished. Why don't we have ourselves a juicy steak, or maybe a roasted homing pigeon?"

His mother nodded and said:

"You're so right, Kiki. How about some simmering shrimp, cream of crab, or clam caramel?"

Mikha'el's grandfather made a face. He hated it when his daughter-in-law called his son by her pet name for him. Oddly, though, Mr. Vitalski's sign caused him to smile with satisfaction. Although Mikha'el himself wouldn't have minded a chicken breast in bread crumbs and some French fries with ketchup, the exchange between his parents worried him. His father had been on a low-cholesterol diet for more than a month, while his mother was so allergic to seafood that a small amount could send her to the hospital. His concern turning to alarm, he glanced at his grandfather, whom he suspected of being behind it all. His grandfather just smiled again.

They entered the restaurant. The décor had changed. A table with five chairs had been placed in the center with the other tables arranged around it in a horseshoe, as though for a birthday party. They stood there uncertainly until Mr. Vitalski deftly ushered them to the center table while whisking away the fifth chair. Mikha'el wondered if it had been meant for Soapy but then proceeded to forget all about her.

Scarcely had they sat down when the restaurant began filling up with customers scurrying to find a seat. They all stared at the Hammermans expectantly. "Let's ignore them," Mikha'el's father suggested while tucking his napkin under his chin.

"They're awfully rude, though," said his mother, spreading her napkin on her lap.

Mikha'el and his grandfather exchanged glances and left their napkins untouched. Grandpa, thought Mikha'el, didn't look like his usual self. He turned to look at the other customers and saw they were changing in front of his eyes. This didn't happen all at once or all together, but something strange was definitely going on.

"Mrs. Salmon, you have a telephone call!" a waiter announced. Although Mikha'el's mother's name was Mrs. Hammerman, she rose and went to the telephone. Mikha'el gave his father a questioning look. There was no response. His father was absorbed in the menu, smiling from time to time while smacking his lips.

"Dad," Mikha'el whispered, "what about your diet?"

His father paid him no attention. Mikha'el glanced at his grandfather, who was reading the menu, too. Or rather, he was pretending to read it, since he had not put on his reading glasses. Meanwhile, the fat man and woman across from them had finished turning into a huge bull and cow. This made no sense, because everyone knew cows were vegetarians and didn't belong in a restaurant on Meat Day. Mikha'el's astonishment grew greater when he saw dark-haired Mr. Shehori, who lived in the house next door to them with his wife and six children, transformed into a giant, menacing crab. It waved its menu with huge pincers and shouted something, its jaws grotesque and its face twitching with feelers.

If Mr. Shehori were boiled in a pot, the unkind thought occurred to Mikha'el, he would turn into a redhead. This made Mikha'el laugh out loud. At once a hush came over the restaurant. All eyes were on him. Although he wanted to jump up and make his getaway, he found he was stuck to his seat. After a moment of panic, he took a deep breath and decided to try again more slowly. First he experimented with lifting a leg. It came up off the floor. Then the other leg—that came up, too. He moved his arms and hands. Everything seemed all right. Yet when he tried rising again, this time with gradual, almost imperceptible movements, his bottom was still glued to the chair. He felt the chair carefully, running his hand over it. Oddly, it was made not from wood but from a smooth, oily substance that clung to him and wouldn't let go of him.

"Dad, can you try getting up for a second?"

This time his father heard him. With a beefy look that Mikha'el had never seen before, he rose from his chair, sat down again, and went back to his menu, beaming more and more broadly. Suddenly, he too was being paged.

"Mr. Roast Beef, telephone!"

Don't go! Mikha'el wanted to scream. His father's name was Mr. Hammerman, not Mr. Roast Beef. But Mikha'el's voice stuck in his throat. Nothing came out but a muffled cry. His father rose and went to the telephone.

Meanwhile, four waiters had arrived with a tray on which lay a gigantic roast goose shaped like a cello. They paraded around the restaurant with it, showing it to all the customers. It was garnished with lace from a dress of his mother's, some fashion magazines, and a musical score. Each customer pointed to the part he or she liked best and the waiters quickly carved it and served it.

"They're eating her," Mikha'el whispered to himself. Out loud he screamed: "You're eating my mom!"

Once again there was silence. The customers regarded him with puzzled looks, as if he had said something either very funny or very foolish. All at once, they began to shout. Their voices were high, low, squeaky, thunderous, not like animal voices at all. Mikha'el couldn't understand a word of it, because geese, ducks, chickens, sheep, pigs, turkeys, doves, partridges, and all their mates and offspring were babbling together, joined by clams, turtles, and snails.

The noisiest, despite their reputation for silence, were the fish. Only now did Mikha'el notice that the restaurant was full of them, all waving their forks in the air. Although fish weren't supposed to breathe out of water, none of them was choking. At least if they were eating his mother, Mikha'el thought with a sigh of relief, she wouldn't have to eat them. "That's a good one," he said to himself, and laughed. "I should tell it to Grandpa." But Grandpa had no time for jokes. He was pointing boisterously at one fish after another while declaiming:

"Trout, carp, mullet, salmon, sole, mackerel, tuna, grouper, sea bass, bonito, cod, sardine, bream, flounder, blenny, bluefish, anchovy, barracuda, sprat, catfish . . ."

Mikha'el gazed at the family of catfish, all with the whiskers of Mr. Eliezer from the photography store. They were sitting on their tails and craning their heads as if these were perched on hidden, rubbery necks. He tried making out what they were shouting, if only a single word. It was impossible.

After a while, the customers quieted down and their last shouts trailed off. There was another hush. Everyone raised his or her fork and knife and stared at the kitchen door. Through it came a new parade of waiters with a tray as big as a table, on which lay a gorgeously browned roast on a bed of bay leaves and rosemary. Topping it off was Mikha'el's father's necktie, with side dishes of contracts, account books, and income tax returns. This time, too, the waiters went from table to table and all the customers picked the cuts of their choice.

"They're eating him, too," Mikha'el whispered to himself, and he screamed out loud:

"You're eating my dad!"

Everything stopped once more. The customers looked up in surprise and began to yell and point, brandishing their silverware and smacking their lips like Mikha'el's father had done over his menu. Mikha'el's heart skipped a beat. He was sure he was next. But he wasn't. Next was Grandpa.

"Mr. Shagface, telephone!"

No! Mikha'el wanted to scream. But Grandpa rose swiftly and walked briskly past the telephone to the kitchen. A minute later he came flying out again to a chorus of disgusted shouts:

"Get out of here, you bony old vegetarian!"

The kitchen staff stood in the doorway, surrounding the chef. Mr. Shagface winked at Mikha'el as he passed him on his way out of the restaurant, which he left with a springy step to the boos of the customers.

"Mr. Eggpoach, telephone!"

The name wasn't even funny. Neither was being called "Mister." The chair released its grip on him, and Mikha'el struggled to his feet. Although he wanted to flee to his grandfather, his legs refused to obey him and took him to the kitchen instead. He stared in horror at the steaming pots and sizzling frying pans, the long carving knives and bread saws. The kitchen staff regarded him delightedly, licking their chops. To his dismay, he saw their faces were changing, too. Noses turned into snouts, teeth grew sharp points, and faces were covered with fur. When all lunged at Mikha'el with outstretched paws, he awoke with a scream.

He jumped out of his grandfather's bed, ran to his parents' bedroom, and—against all the rules—burst in without knocking. His heart was pounding. There was silence. He peered into the darkness. The only light came from the two alarm clocks—his mother's, which stood on his father's side of the bed, and his father's, which stood on his mother's side.

"Dad? Mom?"

They weren't there. Could they really have been eaten? He pinched himself. No, he wasn't dreaming. He ran back to his grandfather's room, shook the old man to wake him, and cried:

"They're gone."

"Who?"

"Mom and Dad."

In the dim, greenish light, Grandpa looked like an evil old wizard. He had taken his false teeth from his mouth and put them in their glass. As Mikha'el stared at them, they lost their wolfishness and became ordinary dentures. He felt his own teeth. Had they also been a wolf's in Grandpa's dream? Had he met his dark side? He didn't think so. As though reading his mind, Grandpa said with a smile:

"Wasn't your father's tie on that roast beef a scream? And those fashion magazines on the goose!"

"Was it a real goose?"

"Unless it was an ostrich. Anyway, they're downstairs watching TV."

Mikha'el jumped up from his grandfather's bed and ran down the stairs. His mother was facing the television, sound asleep.

"Mom!"

He leaped to hug her. Startled, she fended him off.

"I had the scariest dream," he said, trying to remember what had been so frightening.

Mikha'el's father was bent over a plate of frankfurters with mustard and sauerkraut. In the middle of swallowing a mouthful, he nearly choked, until Mikha'el gave him a manly slap on the back. With a sigh of relief, Mikha'el settled into an easy chair. His parents seemed fine to him, no different from usual. His mother glanced at the television, grimaced, and scolded her husband:

"Kiki, what's the matter with you? That's no movie for a child to watch!"

Mikha'el, who had already noticed the R-rated sign, kept his eyes on the screen.

"I can't turn it off in the middle of the suspense," his father said. "Michael, I hope you realize"—his dad always called him by his English name—"that those are just actors making believe. Nothing bad is really happening."

"I know," Mikha'el said. "All that blood is actually ketchup. But why aren't the murders on the evening news R-rated, too?"

"You have a point there," said his father through the frankfurters and sauerkraut. "Maybe you should be the minister of education when you grow up, instead of a sculptor."

"I want to be a vegetarian," Mikha'el said.

"That's all we need," groaned his mother.

"In this world it's eat or be eaten," his father said. "You must have learned about the food chain in school."

"Human beings aren't animals," Mikha'el replied. "No moral person eats meat."

"Who says?" his mother challenged.

"Grandpa."

"Morality has nothing to do with it," said his father, who had forgotten all about the movie.

"Suppose it were the other way around and animals ate people?"

Mikha'el's father chuckled. "Sometimes they do."

"I mean with a knife and fork," Mikha'el said.

His mother shuddered.

"I had a terrible dream that I can't remember," she said. "But I want to ask you, Kiki, to call off that imported meat deal. Invest your money in something else. You promised your father."

"He doesn't suspect a thing."

"He does," Mikha'el's mother said. "He read one of your faxes that I forgot to take out of the machine."

"Damn!" Mikha'el's father said before checking himself.

"I'll eat with Grandpa, and Madame Saupier will cook for us," Mikha'el said.

His mother was exasperated. "Your grandfather is a bad influence. How will you grow bigger if you don't eat meat?"

"Elephants don't eat meat either," Mikha'el said.

His mother turned away from the television and picked up a fashion magazine from the pile on the table. Mikha'el grinned. He glanced at his father's tie. Yes, it was the same. The movie was boring. After watching it for a while, his eyes shut.

His mother kissed him good night and said:

"Go to bed, Miki. You fell asleep in the chair."

"Good night," Mikha'el said to his parents, and slipped off to his grandfather's room. Grandpa was reading in bed.

"Is everything all right?" he asked.

"My mom told my dad to call off the imported meat deal. She said she had an awful dream."

Grandpa smiled. "Excellent! I wasn't sure you knew about it. Your mother just helped me avoid a big fight with your father."

"He only said 'damn,' Grandpa."

"He'll call it off," Mikha'el's grandfather said confidently.

"I'll sleep in my own bed tonight," Mikha'el said.

"Did the dream scare you, Mikha'el?" his grandfather asked. "You weren't meant to be in it."

"You didn't tell me that," said Mikha'el. "You were sleeping when I got into bed with you."

Grandpa gave Mikha'el a kiss and he ran on tiptoe to his room. Madame Saupier was still snoring away.

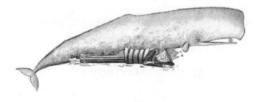

CHAPTER NINE

Wednesday Nights and Ageless Love

WHEN MIKHA'EL'S PARENTS went abroad for a three-week vacation, Madame Saupier agreed to be in charge of him. The first night they were gone she entered the bathroom after he was supposed to have washed and was shocked to discover that all the towels were dry. Her suspicions aroused, she examined the soap and the toothpaste. There was a boy full of germs in the house! Mr. Hammerman might catch some disease.

Madame Saupier hurried to Mikha'el's room. He wasn't there. She found him listening to a story on his grandfather's bed, dragged him back to the bathroom, stuck a toothbrush in his hand, squeezed toothpaste onto it, and made him brush his teeth according to her directions. Then she filled the bathtub and ordered him into it.

"You can't make me."

Madame Saupier thought it over, went to Mikha'el's room, and brought him a bathing suit.

"I'm leaving and when I come back, I expect to find you in the water. If you're not, you're barred from your grandfather's room."

Mikha'el stuck to his guns. The old witch wouldn't tell him what to do.

"You're not my mother and you won't order me around."

"Your parents left me in charge of you. You'll either do what I tell you until they come back or stay away from your grandfather!"

"I'm not taking any baths," Mikha'el declared.

"All right, then. Go to sleep."

Mikha'el went to his room and got into bed, determined not to yield. But he didn't want to miss repair night, either. It was Wednesday. Every Wednesday night, he and his grandfather went on a fix-it trip. Soapy and her bath couldn't have happened at a worse time.

He switched on his reading lamp to keep himself awake and listened to the sounds in the house. Madame Saupier was up and around for a long time. Even after she went to her room, not a snore was heard. She couldn't fall asleep. She had a premonition she couldn't explain. Perhaps it had to do with Mr. Hammerman's failing health, or perhaps with the stubborn, germ-ridden boy she had been left with.

Mikha'el managed to stay awake, pulling himself back from the verge of sleep time after time. At last he heard Soapy snoring.

In the middle of the night she awoke. For a while she lay there, straining to hear a cough or a sneeze from Mr. Hammerman's room. The light coming from the hallway seemed brighter than usual. Getting out of bed, she discovered that Mikha'el had left his bedside lamp on and forgotten to shut his door.

Such an absent-minded boy, she said to herself, and went to switch off Mikha'el's lamp. To her consternation, he was not in his bed.

❖ ❖ ❖

Grandpa and Mikha'el were in the middle of their weekly repair trip, cruising the city in a cartlike contraption that was a cross between a knife grinder and an old sewing machine. Although it had no motor or steering wheel, there was no need to push it. It ran by itself, and wherever it stopped, a large crowd of men, women, and children of all kinds and ages assembled. Sometimes their cats and dogs came, too. All had dreams that they brought to Mikha'el's grandfather for repair. Grandpa opened each dream and Mikha'el couldn't resist peeking at some.

Most of the repairs were simple, with no stitching or patching necessary. Usually, Grandpa would inject a bit of hope into a dream, or paint it a bright color if it was too dark. The harder dreams had to be sudsed and softened. If a dream was poisonous, it called for an antidote or a purgative. Dreams losing their sweetness needed a stabilizer. Some dreams were beautiful but had faded like old carpets that had to be restored. Mikha'el's job was to hold each dream while handing Grandpa his tools and materials, which were kept in the drawers of the cart. He strutted importantly in front of the spectators.

Sometimes they made the rounds of Jerusalem

and sometimes they visited other cities. Now and then they came to places where people spoke foreign languages. His grandfather was never at a loss. When Grandpa was done with each dream, Mikha'el loved to handle it and smell it before returning it to its owner.

Dreams that couldn't be fixed, or were broken or putrid, Grandpa would offer to buy, but if the dreamers wouldn't sell, Grandpa did his best with them. He was shocked when Mikha'el suggested that such dreams be thrown out.

There were also dreams, full of sorrow and longing for lost loved ones whom even dreaming couldn't bring back, that Grandpa handled with special care. Sometimes Mikha'el saw tears in his eyes. Once, they were brought a dream by a young man. It was of a river he had to cross in order to reach the woman he loved. He was never able to swim it.

"Can't you help him, Grandpa?" asked Mikha'el, stricken with sorrow himself.

"The next time he brings us that dream, Mikha'el, take a good look at it."

Mikha'el took a good look the next time and saw that the young man was his grandfather. He recognized him from the old photo albums. When they woke, he said:

"That wasn't someone else's dream, Grandpa. It was yours."

"So it was."

"Who was that girl across the river?"

"My first love."

Mikha'el was disappointed. "You mean we're only fixing our own dreams?"

"No. Most of them are other people's."

"And in the really real world they're fixed?"

"I hope so. It's sometimes possible to know, but rarely."

"How?" Mikha'el asked.

"By asking the dreamer."

"He didn't wash!" Madame Saupier shouted, waking them both in a fright. "This is the last time. From now on he sleeps in his own bed."

"He can sleep with me whenever he has a bad dream," Mr. Hammerman said. "That was our agreement."

"I never agreed to any such thing," Madame Saupier retorted angrily. "I'm responsible for your health and he's old enough to deal with his own fears."

"Suppose," Mikha'el forced himself to ask, "that I wash?"

"Nothing doing!" said Madame Saupier. She turned to Mr. Hammerman. "I can't allow him to sleep so close to you and breathe on you all night long. He'll have to wash just to enter your room."

When Grandpa had said that Madame Saupier would one day make trouble, Mikha'el thought, he had known what he'd been talking about.

Madame Saupier led Mikha'el back to his room, went to the basement, and came back with a folding cot, on which she lay down in front of Mr. Hammerman's door.

For three straight days, Mikha'el couldn't get near his grandfather. He was allowed only to say good morning from the doorway and to get a good-night kiss. Every night he and Madame Saupier had the same conversation.

"Are you going to wash?"

"No."

"At least brush your teeth and clean those filthy feet of yours."

"All right. But first leave."

Madame Saupier would leave, come back, and say:

"You finished too fast. Get back into the tub."

"I won't."

Coming home from school that Wednesday afternoon, Mikha'el heard shouting as he approached the house. He opened the front door apprehensively and found his grandfather in a chair, looking hale and hearty, while Madame Saupier shrieked in despair. His grandfather, it seemed, had stopped washing, too. For the past three days he had refused to brush his teeth, change his socks, or put on his pajamas. At night he slept in his clothes without taking off his shoes.

Mikha'el got the idea. He too stopped changing his clothes, especially his socks. Although he went on combing his hair, brushing his teeth was out of the question. Madame Saupier went about doggedly, her nose plugged with absorbent cotton. She knew she was facing a full-scale rebellion and had no intention of surrendering.

"Are you going to wash tonight, Mikha'el?"

"No."

"I hate to think of what your mother will say when she returns."

Mikha'el's clothes were smellier than his grandfather's. Madame Saupier snatched them and threw them into the washing machine when she could, but Mikha'el tried to outsmart her. Coming home from a long bike ride, for example, he would hide his sweaty shirt beneath his mattress. His smelly socks were stashed there, too. In the end, they gave him away because Madame Saupier sniffed them out. His other clothes he hid in the garden. They didn't remain there long, however, because the gardener, thinking they were rags left by Mrs. Hammerman to clean his tools with, walked off with them. That's when Mikha'el had the bright idea of using his school locker.

"Mikha'el, you stink," a schoolmate said to him after a week had passed. Mikha'el didn't care. He knew what he was doing. Or rather, he thought he knew, because Grandpa still hadn't told him his plan.

Every night when Mikha'el came for his goodnight kiss, his grandfather took a deep whiff of him. On the tenth night he said:

"Perfect!"

✤ ✤ ✤

Mikha'el was asleep when Grandpa threw off the blanket, took his pillow, stepped over Madame Saupier's folding cot, and carefully squeezed into Mikha'el's narrow bed. Mikha'el woke with a start to find his grandfather beside him.

"Grandpa, are you all right?"

"Yes, Mikha'el. Don't worry. Where's your key to the front door?"

"In my school bag."

"Get it."

Mikha'el rose, switched on the bedside lamp, took the key, hung it around his neck as he did when he went to school, and climbed back into bed. Before turning out the light, he took a look at his grandfather. Something protruded from his lips. Wolf's teeth? He turned off the light and lay there anxiously.

Before long, they were walking through the sleeping streets of the city. All of a sudden, Mikha'el noticed that little black creatures were jumping out of garbage cans and sewers and running after them.

"Grandpa, we're being followed."

"So we are," his grandfather replied cheerfully. "They smell us."

Mikha'el bent to look at the scuttling black shapes twitching their feelers and made a nauseated face.

"Grandpa! They're giant black cockroaches."

"En garde, Madame Saupier!" Grandpa chortled. "Tonight you're going to be taught a lesson."

There was a nasty glee in his voice. All at once, Mikha'el caught on and grinned. He ran a finger over his teeth. They felt sharper.

The two of them hurried home, the black bugs in their wake. Some tried climbing up Mikha'el's pajama leg. He shook them off disgustedly and broke into a run. Grandpa kept up with him like a young man and the black bugs scrambled madly after them or took to the air to catch up. Soon they were home.

"Open the door!" Grandpa shouted.

Mikha'el opened the door with his key and the two of them raced inside. The cockroaches hurried after them. Grandpa led them to the second-floor hallway and stopped. He and Mikha'el flattened themselves against a wall and waited. At first nothing happened. The only sound was the ghastly rustle of tiny legs crossing the floor and the splat of roach wings colliding with the walls.

There was a scream. Madame Saupier sprang out of bed so explosively that her folding cot fell to the floor and banged shut. Her hair streaming wildly behind her, she ran down the hallway in her nightshirt, furiously spraying the roaches with a can. Each time she stepped on one with a crunch and a squish, her face twisted with revulsion. Suddenly, she slipped on the oozy floor and fell with a crash. But no—it wasn't Madame Saupier who had fallen. It was Grandpa. The roaches swarmed over him, covering him from head to foot.

"Grandpa!" Mikha'el screamed, terrified. "Get up!"

His scream woke him. Nervously, he felt the bed. Grandpa wasn't in it. The light from the hallway lit the bent figure of Madame Saupier in his room. So that was it: Grandpa had fallen out of bed and the crash had woken her. Mikha'el jumped up and helped her lift his grandfather. Mr. Hammerman stood unsteadily for a moment, then sat on the bed with a loud groan.

"I'm leaving," said Madame Saupier, her arms

crossed on her chest. "And don't think it's because of the bugs."

"I didn't mean to drive you away, Jeanette," Grandpa said. "I just wanted to teach you a lesson. You've become unbearably bossy."

Madame Saupier ignored him and continued. "I was running down the hallway and saw you and all those bugs . . . and then I woke and realized I had been in your dream, Raphael."

Mikha'el saw a tear roll down her cheek.

"To think I believed you when you said you'd lost the gift! What a fool I was. You tricked me. It was a mean thing to do."

"I didn't trick you. I just didn't want to make you unhappy."

"All these years you could have taken me with you in your dreams," Madame Saupier wailed.

In a flash, Mikha'el understood.

"You treated me like a piece of furniture" she went on. "It was convenient for you to have me around. You didn't love me anymore!"

"I treated you like a friend."

"A housekeeper," she said bitterly. "Mr. Raphael Hammerman's kept housekeeper."

"My dreams are my own, Jeanette," Grandpa said.

"I devoted my life to you, and along comes this boy . . ."

"He's my grandson."

Jealousy, Mikha'el remembered his grandfather saying, was the dark side of love.

Grandpa rose from the bed and left the room. Madame Saupier followed him without a word, shaking all over. Before falling asleep, Mikha'el heard her sobs through the shut door. He missed his mother.

Morning light pierced the heavy curtains on the window of his room. Mikha'el jumped out of bed, ran to the hallway, and stopped short. A few squashed insects lay on the floor. They didn't go away when he rubbed his eyes and pinched himself. *A slight distortion of reality,* he thought, regarding them with distaste. He sidestepped them and hurried to his grandfather's room. Grandpa wasn't there. Passing the bathroom on his way back, Mikha'el heard someone in the shower.

"Grandpa?"

Mr. Hammerman didn't hear because the water drowned out Mikha'el's voice. Mikha'el went to the kitchen to see if Madame Saupier had made breakfast. No one was there. Dead bugs littered the floor. He ran to her room. The door was shut and there was no answer when he knocked. He hesitated, then pressed the door handle and entered. The room was empty. He went to the closet and opened it. Madame Saupier's clothes were gone. Turning around, he saw his grandfather standing in the doorway in a bathrobe.

"Grandpa, she's gone."

"I know."

"Because of the bugs?"

"No."

"Then why?"

His grandfather sighed.

"From heartbreak. She realized I wasn't in love with her anymore."

"How could you have been in love?" Mikha'el wondered. "Grandpa, you're two old people."

"Someday you'll understand. Love is ageless."

Grandpa made Mikha'el hot chocolate and some bread spread with cheese and a slice of tomato. Usually, Mikha'el had coffee with a piece of French toast for breakfast, but this morning he had no appetite. Every bite he took felt like the squish of a bug between his teeth. His grandfather made him a sandwich for school. It looked strange, but Mikha'el took it. He went to his bedroom, shouldered his school bag, and walked gingerly down the stairs. A few black bugs by the front door ran for cover. Mikha'el ignored them. He could still hear the splatter of them beneath poor Madame Saupier's shoes. Gently, he shut the door behind him.

He was too upset to concentrate in class. He could barely hear or answer the teacher's questions. All he could think of was his grandfather, alone in the house. When the last bell rang, Mikha'el raced home. There wasn't a sign of the cockroaches. The house was as spick-and-span as if Madame Saupier were still there.

"I ordered a cleaning crew and an exterminator," Grandpa explained.

That evening Grandpa invited Mikha'el to eat in Mr. Yerek's vegetarian restaurant. Although Mikha'el was scared, his grandfather explained that they would dine in the really real world. In fact, they would eat all their meals there until a new housekeeper was found.

"All right," Mikha'el said warily.

All went well. True, there was a new sign on the door in big black letters, but all it said was:

FRESH PAINT

And yet, Mikha'el thought, *how odd.*

"Grandpa, do you remember the color of that door in our dream?"

"It was green," his grandfather said. "Just like it is now."

"That's right. But before that, in the really real world in which we came here with Madame Saupier, it was white."

"That could well be," Grandpa said matter-of-factly.

In the days before his parents returned from abroad, Mikha'el watched R-rated movies every evening on television. Usually, he fell asleep in front of the screen and had to be woken by his grandfather, who sent him off to brush his teeth and go to bed.

When his parents walked in the door, he gave his mother a big hug.

"Did you miss me?" she asked.

"Did you bring me a present?" asked Mikha'el.

"We'll unpack in a minute," his father said. "Where's Madame Saupier?"

They could hardly believe that she had left after a quarrel with Grandpa.

"How will you manage without her?" asked Mikha'el's father.

"I've already called an employment agency and asked for a housekeeper, a cook, and a caretaker for an old man. The candidates are coming tomorrow. I hope you'll help me choose."

Grandpa smiled.

Mikha'el's mother smiled back.

When they unpacked, they gave Mikha'el a little steam engine with a real boiler, a pressure gauge, an overflow pipe, and a manual pressure release. The steam whistled like an old locomotive. There was a place for a fire beneath the boiler, a steam-propelled flywheel, and a piston-operated miniature crane.

"When your father was a small boy, Grandpa bought him a steam engine like this," Mikha'el's mother said. "We were thrilled to find one just like it."

Mikha'el ran to give his father a big hug, too.

CHAPTER TEN

The Dream Key

As Mr. Hammerman's health grew worse, his dreams changed. They had fewer adventures and exotic voyages and more memories. In them, Mikha'el felt like a bystander witnessing a scene he has chanced to come across. Sometimes the dreams were exciting. Other times, Mikha'el was scared to death—as he was by Grandpa's war memories, for instance, with their contorted faces and shrieks of pain. After waking from those dreams, Mikha'el would go off to sleep in his own room. Days, sometimes weeks, might go by before he joined his grandfather for another dream.

One night he woke up from a nightmare in his own bed and ran to his grandfather's room. Although the bedside lamp was lit and Grandpa still had his reading glasses on, his open book had fallen onto his chest.

"What's the matter, Mikha'el? What did you dream?"

"I dreamed that Soapy was chasing me with a mouth full of wolf's teeth."

Grandpa laughed. For the first time in a long while, he moved over to make room for Mikha'el in his bed. "I'm glad you came," he said. "It's Wednesday. We don't have much time."

"Are you going away, Grandpa?"

"No. Not yet."

"But you don't have that much longer to live, do you?"

"No," Mr. Hammerman said.

"Grandpa, are you dying?"

Grandpa laughed. "Not right now."

They set out in their repair cart. Grandpa looked big and strong, the picture of health. What happened next was unexpected. A girl Mikha'el's age tugged at his shirt and asked him to sweeten a dream. Mikha'el didn't know what to do. Although he thought he should direct her to his grandfather, Grandpa was signaling him to fix her dream himself.

"But . . ."

Grandpa handed him a large iron key.

"Sweeten her dream," he said.

Mikha'el went to work and sweetened the dream as best he could. When he returned it, the girl let out a laugh that he recognized. It was Maya's. Then he woke up.

It was morning. Mikha'el wasn't surprised to wake up in his grandfather's bed. The strange thing was that one of his hands was curled into a fist and had something hard in it. Mikha'el opened it and saw the key. He turned it this way and that. It was smaller than the key in the dream and notched on both sides.

"Grandpa?"

His grandfather lay beside him with open eyes.

"Look! I've still got the key."

"I know," Grandpa said.

Mikha'el held out his hand to return it.

"No, Mikha'el. It's yours now."

"But Grandpa, won't you need it in your dreams?"

"Not anymore."

"Where did you get it?"

"My father gave it to me when he saw I had the gift, just as I've seen that you have it."

"Does my dad have the gift, too?"

"Your father? No, he doesn't."

"How come?"

"It's not his fault. He just wasn't born with it. He lives too much in the really real world."

Grandpa looked hard at Mikha'el. "I know what you're thinking. But the key wouldn't help him any. I always wished he were different, too, but I got over it when I met you."

"Did you know as soon as you saw me?"

"No. There's no knowing for sure. But I did have a feeling about you. As a boy, I was like you."

"Not like the other boys?"

"No. Different."

Mikha'el fell silent. He was thinking of the dream.

"That girl was Maya, from my class."

The name didn't ring a bell to Grandpa.

"Don't you remember? She's in my sculpture club at the museum. I fixed her bike."

Now Mr. Hammerman recalled. "Did she recognize you?"

"I think so. She looked at me and laughed."

"If it really was her, she may remember the dream, too."

Mikha'el was alarmed. "What happens then?"

Mr. Hammerman sat solemnly up in bed.

"What is it, Grandpa?"

"If she does, that's proof that you have the gift."

Mikha'el had never been so impatient to get to school as he was that morning.

"What's the big rush?" his mother asked.

He was in too much of a hurry to answer her, let alone kiss her goodbye, and he totally forgot about his father. He ran all the way. As he did, he kept thinking of how to approach Maya. He couldn't do it in class. The boys would laugh at him for the rest of the year.

Just then he saw her, walking with her friends on the other side of the street. He stopped in his tracks. What now? At that very moment, Maya turned her head, caught sight of him, and stopped, too. Her friends didn't notice and kept skipping gaily down the street. Without thinking twice, Mikha'el crossed to her side. The closer he came to her, the more nervous he felt. Before he could open his mouth, Maya smiled shyly and said:

"Mikha'el . . ."

She blushed, not finding the words.

"What were you going to say?" he asked.

She glanced at her receding friends. "Do you swear not to laugh at me?"

"I swear."

"Or tell your friends?"

"Never."

"Or anyone?"

"Or anyone." To himself he added: *Except Grandpa.*

"I had a strange dream that you were in. You were driving a cart that looked like an old sewing machine."

"Maya!" her friends called to her, noticing she had lagged behind. She left Mikha'el and ran to catch up with them.

School seemed to last forever. Worse yet, Maya's friends kept staring at him while whispering and giggling. Maya, on the other hand, didn't look his way once. Even before the last bell had rung, all his things were back in his school bag. He raced home at top speed, threw the bag onto the floor, sprinted up the stairs, and burst into his grandfather's room.

"Grandpa! She said she did! She said she did!"

"Did what?"

Mikha'el was panting so hard that he had to stop to catch his breath.

"Grandpa, she said she dreamed about me."

His grandfather signaled Mikha'el to come to him and sat him on his knees. "Well!" he said. "You couldn't have asked for a better sign that you're on your way to becoming a dream master."

"I'm not one already?"

"No, not yet. But you will be when you grow up."

"How do you know, Grandpa?"

"Because that slight distortion of reality last night was your own doing. I was with you, but I had nothing to do with it."

"Was it the key?"

"I've already told you. The key has no power in itself. It has to be in the hands of the right person."

"Suppose I lose it?" he asked anxiously.

"You can't. You and the key are inseparable now."

Mikha'el felt very proud. He gave Grandpa a hug and kissed his cheek, even though he knew the bristles would scratch him.

CHAPTER ELEVEN
The Really Real World

GRANDPA DREAMED AGAIN of the house. Mikha'el saw
a couple standing near it. At once he recognized the
pair as his grandfather and the girl across the river in
the dream that couldn't be fixed. It was snowing and
they both wore winter coats. The house had changed.
It had only two floors and it faced not a street but a
dirt road planted with several palm trees. The neighborhood had also changed. There were fewer houses,
each with an unobstructed view of the old city wall.
It was very dark out. The house was dark, too, except
for some candles burning in the entrance. The snow

covered everything—the palm trees and the city wall, too. The young couple held hands, foreheads touching. For a long while, they stood there without speaking or moving. Mikha'el wondered whether Grandpa had had the gift of taking his loved ones into his dreams even then. The snow kept falling in large flakes. Mikha'el scooped some to make a snowball.

He awoke with cold hands. Jumping out of his grandfather's bed, he ran to look at them by the glow of the light in the hallway. Not all of the snow had melted. He licked it with his tongue.

Grandpa woke, too, and switched on the light by his bed. Mikha'el ran back to show him his hands.

"They're wet," said his grandfather, touching them.

"It's snow, Grandpa!"

Mr. Hammerman put on his reading glasses and looked at the snowflakes, which were rapidly turning into water. He smiled as one smiles at a sweet memory of first love. Then he asked Mikha'el to wake his caretaker and ask her to cover his feet with the electric blanket, because they were cold. In the really real world, it was still summer.

✻ ✻ ✻

After the night of that dream, Mr. Hammerman no longer left his bed. Mikha'el looked in on him every day after school.

"How are you feeling, Grandpa?"

"Not so good. Have a seat and read me the newspaper."

Every evening Mikha'el came to kiss Grandpa good night. When Grandpa shut his eyes, he reminded Mikha'el of the dead people he'd seen on television. Mikha'el wished he hadn't talked him out of using his anti-time machine.

They were flying over a ravishing mountain landscape. Something was squeaking on his grandfather's bicycle.

"What a strange time of day," Mr. Hammerman said when they landed at night among some tall trees. They dismounted and walked slowly to a house standing in a woods. The entrance was lit, and steps led to a front door that was open. A room was visible inside. Mikha'el recognized the scene right away. Now, too, some people sat on the steps, while others stood in the entrance or looked out the window of the room.

"Grandpa, we've been here before."

His grandfather nodded. He was very pale. With a single look that had no words or gestures, he was asked to enter the house. His bicycle fell apart and vanished into the carpet of pine needles on the ground.

"Mikha'el! My bicycle is gone and I can't wake up."

"Grandpa," Mikha'el shouted, "don't wake up! Whatever you do, don't wake up now!"

His grandfather gave him an earnest look.

"All right," he said.

"Grandpa . . ."

Mikha'el burst into tears.

Mr. Hammerman's funeral took place in the really real world. There was a large crowd. Mikha'el stood between his father and his mother, who hugged him anxiously. But he wasn't anxious himself. He knew that his grandfather was in the dream of the lit house in the dark woods and that he could visit him there whenever he could find it. There were many things he wanted to tell him. The first was that Madame Saupier had come to the funeral and had fallen weeping on the grave after the gravediggers had piled earth on top of it. Grandpa's family, who had gathered from all over the country, shook their heads and smiled with a mixture of sympathy and spite. Mikha'el smiled, too. For some reason, he thought of his grandfather's knowing wink.

When the funeral was over, Madame Saupier came forward to shake his parents' hands and give him a hug. He submitted to it good-naturedly.

"What's that in your hand?" his father asked.

Mikha'el opened his fist, revealing the key. His father took it and studied it.

"Why, it's the key to Grandpa's old house," he marveled.

"Grandpa gave it to me," Mikha'el said warily.

"Keep it," said his father. "It's a nice souvenir."

Mikha'el kept the key. Each time he held it up to his ear, he heard the song of the whales.